If It's Snowy and You Know It, Clap Your Paws!

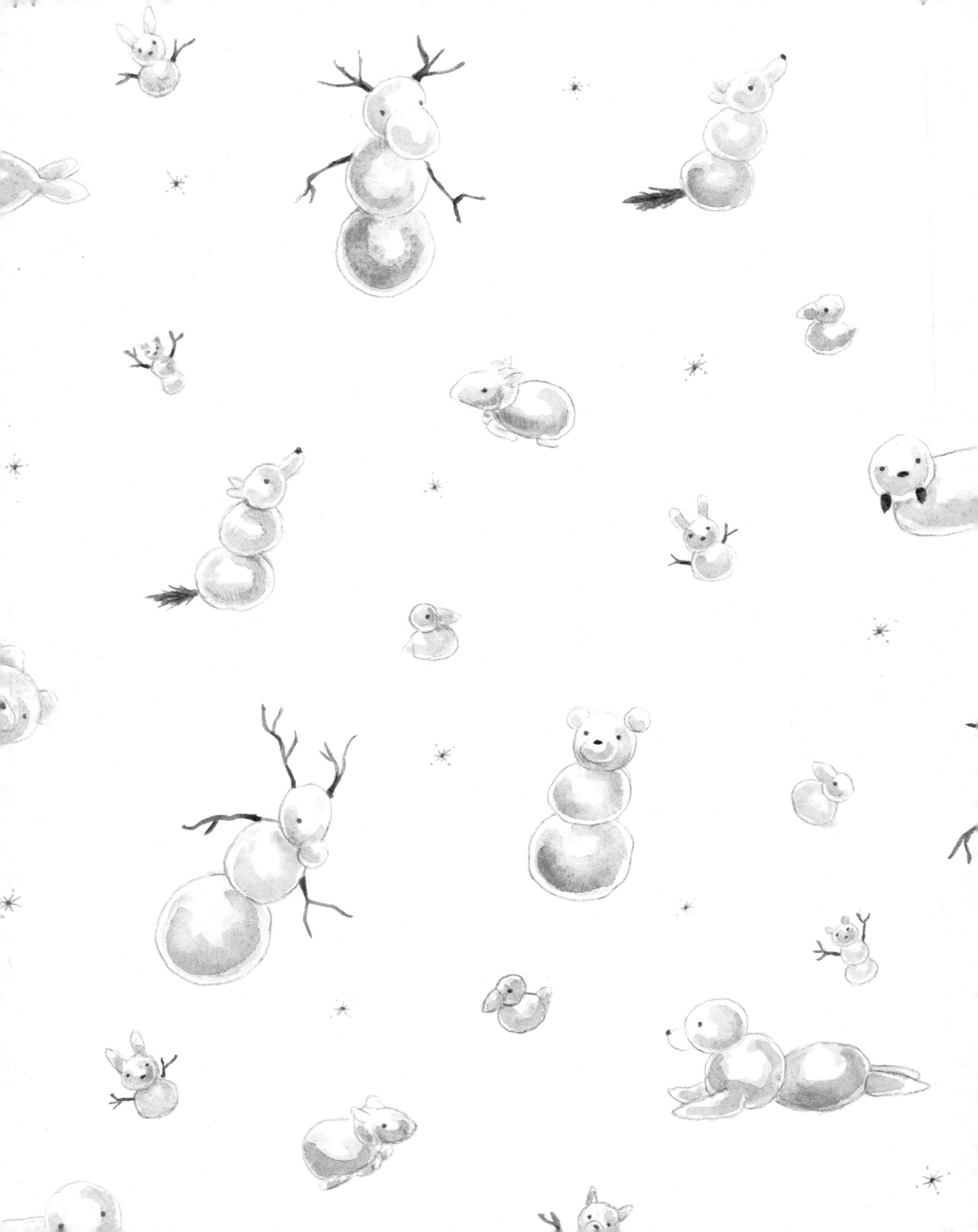

For Beth Ann, Sean, and Eric,
grand niece and nephews, indeed! –K.N.

For Thomas and Edie –L.W.

ISBN 978-0-545-67387-7

12 11 10 9 8 7 6 5 4 16 17 18/0

Printed in the U.S.A. 40

First Scholastic printing, December 2013

Designed by Elizabeth Phillips
The illustrations were created using watercolor, colored pencil, and pastel.

If It's Snowy and You Know It, Clap Your Paws!

by
Kim Norman

illustrated by
Liza Woodruff

SCHOLASTIC INC.

If it's snowy and you know it, clap your paws.
You can tumble on the tundra, just because.
If it's snowy and you know it,
roll a snowball up and throw it.
If it's snowy and you know it...

...clap your paws!

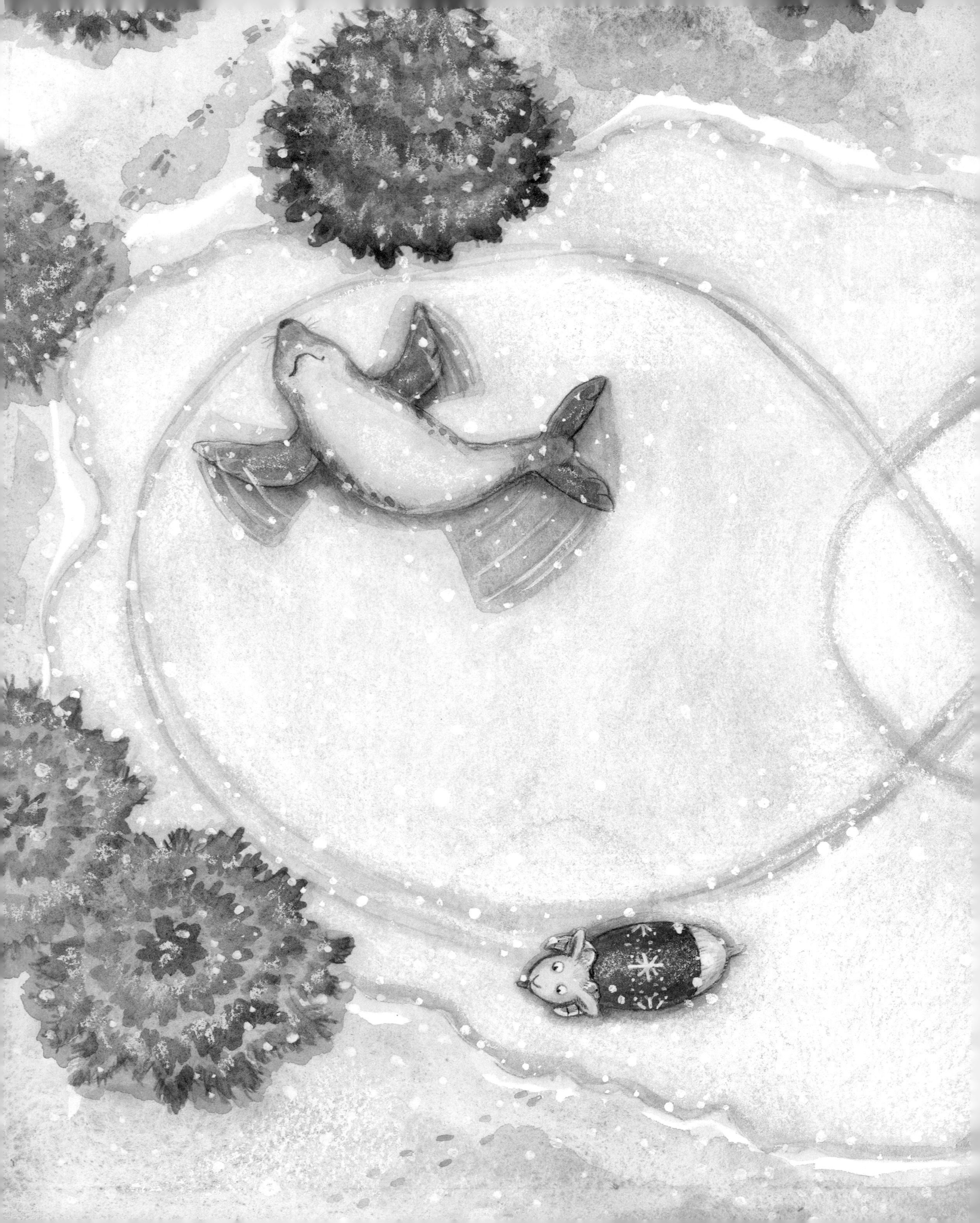

If your fur is full of flurries, taste a flake.
Skate around or make some angels on a lake.
If your fur is full of flurries,
you'll forget your winter worries.
If your fur is full of flurries...

...taste a flake!

CRASH

If the skies are crisp and clearing, grab your skis.
Give your tiny friends a ride behind your knees.
If the skies are crisp and clearing,
let a walrus do the steering.
If the skies are crisp and clearing...

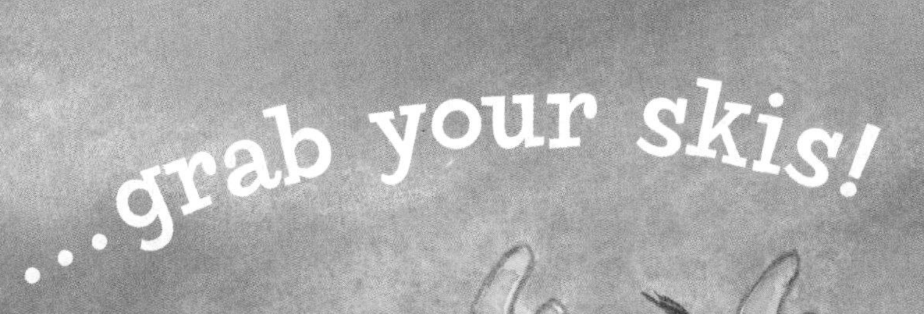
...grab your skis!

If it's shimmery and sunny, sculpt a friend.
If he topples, it's an easy job to mend.
If it's shimmery and sunny,
borrow glasses from the bunny.
If it's shimmery and sunny...

...sculpt a friend!

If it's frosty and you're freezing, build a fort,
leaving room for all your buddies, tall or short.
If it's frosty and you're freezing,
add some curtains that are pleasing.
If it's frosty and you're freezing...

. . . build a fort!

If it's drafty and you're drifting, give a roar.
Get some help from white belugas off the shore.
If it's drafty and you're drifting,
hail a whale for heavy lifting.
If it's drafty and you're drifting...

...give a roar!

If at last you're finally landing, blow a kiss.
Make a promise that you'll write to friends you'll miss.
If at last you're finally landing,
leave the float you've been commanding.
If at last you're finally landing...

...blow a kiss!

If it's starry and you're starving, share a meal.
There's enough for all, from caribou to seal.
If it's starry and you're starving,
add a sparkly iceberg carving.
If it's starry and you're starving...

...share a meal!

If it's arctic and you're aching, soak your toes.
Hold a steamy cup of cocoa to your nose.
If it's arctic and you're aching,
give your paws a gentle baking.
If it's arctic and you're aching…

. . . soak your toes.

If it's wintry and you're weary, go inside.
Paint a picture of the icy sports you tried.
If it's wintry and you're weary,
read a book that's warm and cheery.
If it's wintry and you're weary...

…go inside.

If it's sleeting and you're sleepy, climb in bed.
Tuck your tails and paws and fins beneath the spread.
If it's sleeting and you're sleepy,
snuggle up with something sheepy.
There's a world of wild adventures...

. . . in your head!

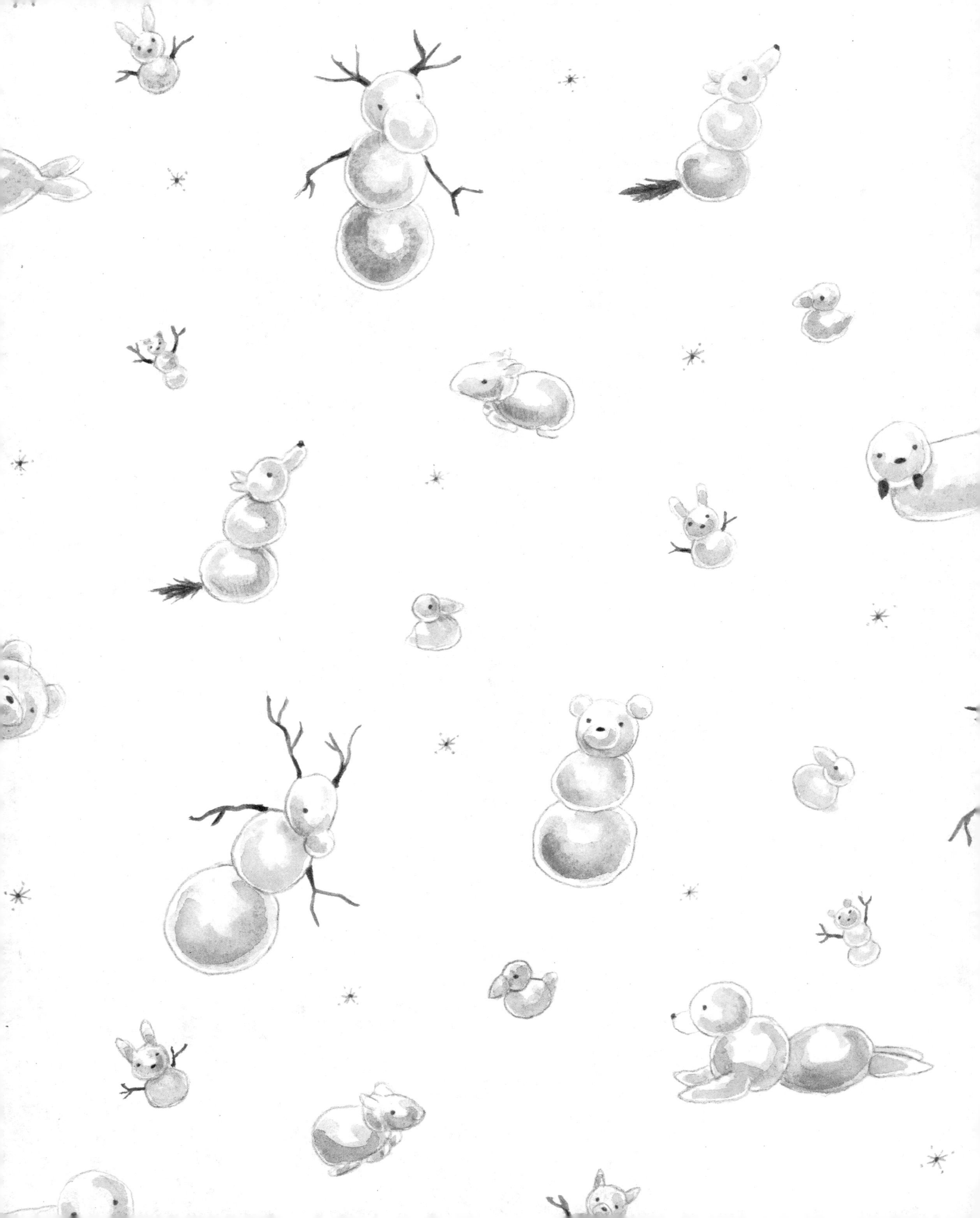